W9-BAK-898

World of Reading

LEVEL 1

THIS IS CAPTAIN AMERICA

Adapted by Brooke Dworkin

Interior illustrated by Val Semeiks, Bob McLeod,
Hi-Fi Design, *and the* Storybook Art Group

Cover illustrated by Val Semeiks *and* Hi-Fi Design

Based on the Marvel comic book series Captain America

ABDO
Spotlight

MARVEL
Los Angeles
New York

ABDOPUBLISHING.COM

Reinforced library bound edition published in 2018 by Spotlight, a division of ABDO, PO Box 398166, Minneapolis, Minnesota 55439. Spotlight produces high-quality reinforced library bound editions for schools and libraries. Published by Marvel Press, an imprint of Disney Book Group.

Printed in the United States of America, North Mankato, Minnesota.
042017
092017

marvelkids.com

THIS BOOK CONTAINS
RECYCLED MATERIALS

© 2014 MARVEL

LIBRARY OF CONGRESS CATALOGING-IN-PUBLICATION DATA

This title was previously cataloged with the following information:

Dworkin, Brooke.
This is Captain America / adapted by Brooke Dworkin ; interior illustrated by Val Semeiks, Bob McLeod, Hi-Fi Design, and the Storybook Art Group ; cover illustrated by Val Semeiks and Hi-Fi Design.
  p. cm. -- (World of reading. Level 1)
Summary: Introduces Captain America, explaining how he came to be a superhero.
1. Captain America (Fictitious character)--Juvenile fiction. 2. Superheroes--Juvenile fiction. 3. America, Captain (Fictitious character) 4. Superheroes.
PZ7.D9625 Th 2014
[E]--dc23
      2014378996

978-1-5321-4051-8 (Reinforced Library Bound Edition)

Spotlight
A Division of ABDO
abdopublishing.com

This is Steve Rogers.

Steve is a soldier.
His friends think he is
weak and clumsy.

Steve was not always strong.

But Steve has a secret.
He is not
what he seems.

Steve is really Captain America!
His friends call him Cap.

When Steve was a young man,
the country went to war.

The war upset people.

They wanted to help.

Steve wanted to help, too.

He decided to join the army.

First a doctor
had to examine him.
Steve waited a long time.

Finally, it was his turn.

The doctor looked
at Steve's eyes.
He listened
to his heart.

Then he took Steve
to his office.

The doctor told Steve
that he was not
fit enough to fight.

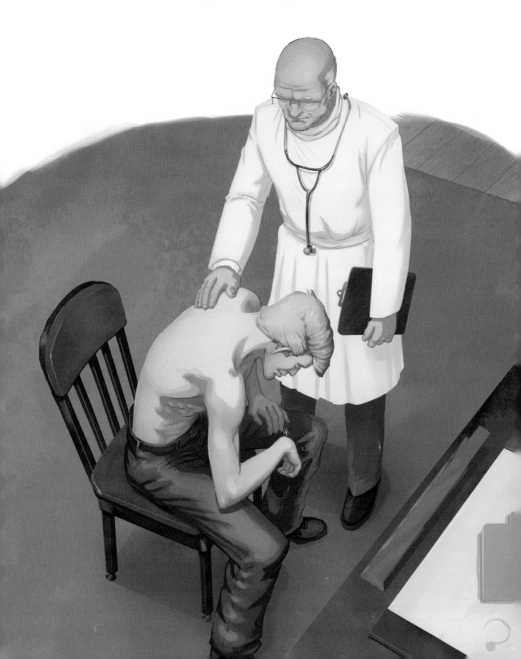

But there was another way
to join the army.

The doctor told Steve about
a top secret project.

In a secret lab,
Steve met Doctor Erskine.

The doctor gave Steve
a special shot.

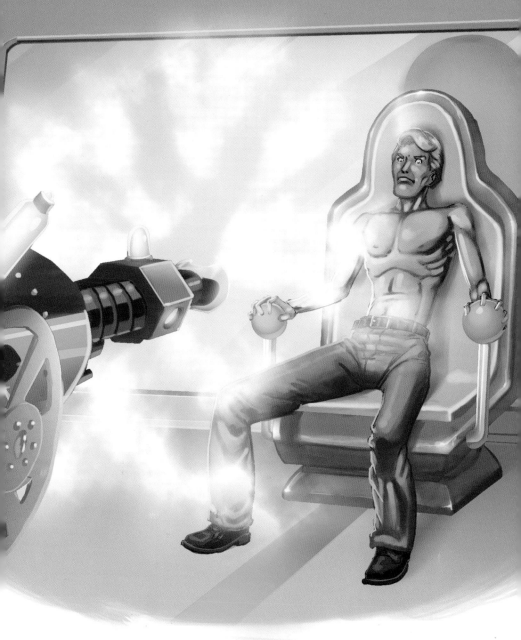

He hit him with
energy rays.

The rays made Steve strong.

The experiment was a success.

Now Steve was healthy enough
to join the army.

The army gave him
a special shield
and a costume.

Steve became Cap.

Now Steve fights enemies
all over the world.
He is the country's best soldier.

Cap is a hero.

BUGLE FINAL
DAILY NEWSPAPER

TANK NO MATCH FOR CAP!

BUGLE FINAL
ILY NEWSPAPER

UGLE FINAL
SPAPER

News Notes
Happenings
DAILY
FINAL

CAP RECEIVES HIGHEST HONOR

News Notes
Happenings

He fights for justice,
equality, and freedom.

And he will never stop!